The Last Train to Clarksville

Sharon Marie Provost

Cover and interior images public domain via Pixabay.
Cover design by Stephen H. Provost.

ISBN: 978-1-949971-61-3

"True love stories never have endings."

— _Richard Bach
"Running from Safety:
An Adventure of the Spirit"

"Life is eternal, and love is immortal, and death is only a horizon; and a horizon is nothing save the limit of our sight.."

— _Rossiter Worthington Raymond

Contents

I.

Sabrina rubbed her temples as she stared out the window of her room at the bed and breakfast, trying to understand what she was feeling. This was supposed to be a simple vacation to unwind and have fun before her life got more complicated. Instead, her life—her feelings—had become just that: more complicated than ever.

Sabrina had had her life all planned out since she was ten years old. To say she was dedicated and hardworking—one might even say single-minded in her determination—was an understatement. She'd had her career picked out by the time she was ten, and she dove into her pursuit of that dream headfirst. She didn't spend her time socializing with other children, and she did not have time for frivolous dates in her teenage years. Boys were just a distraction. The only extracurricular activities she pursued after her schoolwork were those she thought would help her get into the perfect undergrad program... and then the right medical school.

Her mom had been diagnosed with stomach cancer when Sabrina was only five. She didn't have a fun-loving, playful, cookie-baking mother like the other young girls at school. That's not to say that her mother didn't love her and spend endless hours of quality time with her: They read books together, watched educational TV shows, discussed Sabrina's future, and delved into all her little girl dreams, some silly and others surprisingly focused.

Her mom was often tired, nauseated, and in pain. She just didn't have the energy to do all the physical activities that most mothers did, but that was fine with Sabrina because she loved their discussions. It made her feel like an adult, mature and wise, when they talked about life.

All that changed though, when her mother passed away shortly before her 10th birthday. Sabrina had never felt so out of control, and she hated that feeling. There should have been some way to save her mother. The doctors just hadn't thought of it. If Sabrina had been in charge, things would have been different, she was sure.

Her father was a good parent, but he was overwhelmed with his grief, busy at his corporate job, and had no idea how to connect with his daughter the way her mother had. Sabrina's feeling of helplessness and guilt over not being able to save her mother, along with her further isolation, fed her strong-willed determination to excel in school and in pursuing her career. A relationship and children were never in her plan for the future.

Now, she feared all these plans were in jeopardy. She was on track to graduate summa cum laude in the spring with a degree in biology and a pre-med emphasis. She'd been accepted to the best medical school in the country, where she was set to start in eight months. In just a week, during winter break, she was about to start a highly sought-after two-week externship with Dr. Stephens, the head of the Emergency Department at the hospital that worked in tandem with the medical school. This would be an excellent opportunity to make connections and get a leg up on her studies. With any luck, she'd resume working with Dr. Stephens in the summer before she started medical school.

The last thing in the world she had time for was a relationship. But yet, she was contemplating just that. And not just a relationship, but a serious long-distance one. How could this have happened? What was she thinking? Just as important, did he feel the same way? They—or at least she thought both of them—had just experienced the best week of their lives.

"Soulmates" had always seemed like such a stupid concept. It was simply people deluding themselves into thinking they had found their perfect match.

Yet here she was thinking about soulmates.

It had all started last week when she boarded the train to Clarksville. She had always loved trains, so she'd planned a two-day trip by rail to her childhood friend's B&B for some much-needed relaxation. She had paid for a private sleeper car, but there had been a glitch in the reservation system. So instead, she had been booked to share a car with another passenger.

She had protested at first, but the man seemed so nice and desperate to make this trip now.

He boarded the train with his belongings in hand and sheepishly poked his head into the car.

"Miss, where would you like me to stow these? I promise not to be a bother. I really appreciate you letting me share this car with you. I have a lot on my mind right now, and this is my last chance to get away before everything changes."

Sabrina looked up at him. "I was thinking we could each take a side so we can stretch out tonight, and we each get a window that way to see the scenery. So put your belongings anywhere you want across from me. Does that work for you?"

"Yes, Miss. Thank you again. By the way, my name is Jeremiah."

"Nice to meet you, Jeremiah. I am Sabrina."

Both of them settled in quietly and began to read, Jeremiah perusing the *New York Times* and *Wall Street Journal* while Sabrina reviewed her emergency procedures book. Sabrina soon realized they were both spending more time enjoying the scenery than reading.

After a while, Jeremiah excused himself, and before long, Sabrina's curiosity about the train grew—as did her appetite—so she decided to explore a bit before heading to the dining car. She walked the length of the train and spoke briefly with the conductor before stopping in the lounge car. Its large, beautiful windows were perfect for sightseeing, so she decided to stop and have a drink while enjoying the view.

Sabrina ordered a Cosmopolitan from the bar and got a candy bar from the snack bar before she sat down to enjoy the scenery as the train wound its way through the rolling fields. She could just see the mountains in the distance and hoped they would reach them before nightfall. She was trying to identify the many birds she saw flying through the field when she was startled by a voice behind her.

"Would you like some company?"

She looked up to see Jeremiah standing beside her with a beer in hand. She smiled brightly and said, "Sure. That would be lovely."

He sat down across from her. "What are you looking at?"

"I was just doing some bird watching. My mother and I used to do that on weekends—before she got too ill, that is. Uhh... those mountains in the distance are absolutely gorgeous. I hope we reach them while the sun is still out."

"I do hope your mother is better," Jeremiah said. "I wish my parents had spent time with me like that."

Sabrina looked down quickly as a tear slid down her cheek. She turned her head back to the window and carefully wiped it away. Then she met his eyes slowly and said, "My mother passed away from cancer when I was a child."

"I am so very sorry. That was stupid of me to say. Please excuse me," Jeremiah said hurriedly as he moved to get up.

"No, no, no. Don't be ridiculous. You couldn't have known. You were just being polite. Let's talk about you a little. You said when you arrived that you had a lot on your mind and things were about to change. What did you mean—that is, if you don't mind me asking?"

"Well, I just graduated with my master's degree in architecture. I am all set to start at my father's firm next month. But first, I'm taking this trip to clear my head. I have some big decisions to make that will affect my entire future."

"Wow. What kind of big decisions?"

"My family is old money. They have certain expectations about where I work, who my friends are, who I will marry and when... even where I'll live. I have been dating the daughter of my father's best friend since sophomore year of undergrad. Don't get me wrong. Amber is a very sweet girl, beautiful and giving. She will make a wonderful wife... but not for me. We just have different plans in life. She is ready to settle down, have children, and join the boards of local charities. I am serious about my career, but I want to live too. I want to explore the world, ride trains, spend time with friends, and eventually have the 'white picket fence.' My family has already picked out the house they want to gift us as a wedding present. As I said, my start date at my father's firm has already been chosen, but it took a lot of cajoling to negotiate that precious month of freedom. My parents think I just have cold feet, so I'm taking this time to prepare for my engagement. I don't want to disappoint my family, but I'm not sure that I am ready to accept that life. God, look at me going on and on. I'm sure I am boring you. I apologize."

Sabrina felt for him. She could see the stress on his face. Oddly enough, she found she could understand his feelings even though she was on a direct, career-driven path. She wasn't interested in traveling and spending time with friends, but at the same time, she didn't want to be saddled with a spouse and children. She couldn't bear the thought of someone interfering with her path in life.

"I am very sorry, Miss... uh, I mean Sabrina. I don't know what is going on with me today. I'm not usually so talkative, or open, but I just feel so comfortable with you: this instant connection that I can't explain. Shit! Now I just sound stupid, or better yet, creepy. I will just shut up now. I appreciate your kindness in listening to me. I should go."

"Wait! It is OK, really... Now, I should try some of that open honesty. It is more than just OK. I feel the same way. Do I seem like the kind of person who just lets strangers, let alone men, stay in my private sleeper car? I just had this sense about you. Please, sit down and relax."

Jeremiah settled back in his seat with a small smile on his face. Sabrina was looking down, trying to hide the bright red blush on her face.

"Thank you. I appreciate your kind words. Now why don't you tell me more about yourself."

"Well, I just want to say that I don't blame you for your reluctance to follow your family's plan. I'm very independent myself, and I want to make my own decisions about life. While I am very different than you when it comes to my life plan, I would not accept anybody making plans for me."

"How is your plan different?"

"Well, for starters, I will be graduating with my bachelor's degree in biology this spring. I've already been accepted into my dream medical school, and I will be starting in the fall. Next week, I begin a short externship over the winter break that will resume over the summer. My goal is to graduate top of my class, pass my boards in the 90th percentile, become Chief Resident and, ultimately, the youngest Chief of Emergency Medicine in the history of the hospital. I'd love to do research and publish in medical journals. With all that, I just don't have time for a relationship or a family. I am a very career-oriented person."

"I can see that. I don't think I have heard of anyone planning so far ahead in such detail. I respect that though. You know what you want, and you don't intend to let anyone, or anything, get in your way. Does your family support you? "

"My father and grandparents tell me that "every person needs someone to love and support them." They think I will live to regret my decision, and by then, it will be too late to start a family. My father finds it hard to discuss serious topics; he always left that to my mother when I was young. My grandparents just want me to be happy, so they will support me no matter what. That doesn't mean that they don't periodically express their opinion, hoping I will change my mind. I just feel strongly that you should be able to choose how you want to live your life. If traveling and spending time with friends enjoying life is what gives you pleasure, then you should pursue that. You didn't say you're opposed to marriage or a family, just not now and not with her. That is your right."

Jeremiah smiled brightly, showing a genuine sense of relief. He took a deep breath before quietly asking if Sabrina wanted to join him for dinner in the dining car. Sabrina readily agreed: She was utterly famished after such a deep but satisfying conversation. Besides, she wanted to spend more time with Jeremiah.

They each ordered a rib-eye steak, medium-well; loaded baked potatoes (minus the butter); and broccolini. They enjoyed a bottle of Cabernet Sauvignon while they waited for dinner to arrive.

"This will sound silly, but I was shocked when our orders matched," Sabrina said.

Jeremiah laughed heartily and exclaimed, "You mean the butter."

Sabrina nodded her head eagerly.

"Whenever I order my potato that way, people always comment, 'Who doesn't like butter? Who doesn't want butter on their baked potato?' Me, that's who! The butter takes away from the flavor of the sour cream, cheese, and bacon. If I am having a regular baked potato, then butter, and lots of it, is great."

"But loaded is different. I totally agree."

Before they knew it, the hour was late, and the dining car serving staff was cleaning up for the night, so Sabrina and Jeremiah retired to their sleeper car to continue their conversation. Neither one of them was tired yet.

The topic of conversation ranged from politics to TV shows (their shared guilty pleasure lay in watching reality romance shows like 90 Day Fiancé and Married at First Sight) and even their favorite music (they both adored Fleetwood Mac and The Beatles).

They were fascinated by their many similarities, which they continued to explore as the conversation continued deep into the night. As they began to get tired, they set up bedding on their respective seats and continued enjoying each other's company: It was like an adult slumber party.

Sometime past 3, the conversation slowed naturally as they fought to keep their eyes open. Neither one knew who fell asleep first, but they both awoke shortly after 9 a.m. when they heard the other passengers moving noisily through the narrow passageway.

"Well good morning, Sunshine."

Sabrina giggled happily. "I have never had that much fun before. I didn't have many close friends as a child. I spent a lot of quality time with my mother, helping care for her until she passed when I was 10. Then I kind of retreated into myself and my schoolwork, so I just didn't create those bonds. I never had the slumber party experience with girlfriends like that, talking and laughing all night. Thank you very much!"

"Shall we get dressed and go get some grub?"

"Yes, please! I am so hungry I could eat a whole pig... all the bacon. In fact, I just might. In case you haven't noticed, I am a bit of a carnivore. I know, I know. Here I am studying to be a doctor, and I should know better about eating red meat. But come on! You only live once, and I will not settle for anything less. Down with the turkey bacon! That shit is not bacon. Please pardon my French."

Jeremiah burst out laughing. He seemed delighted with her sense of humor. She'd had fun last night, but she hadn't let herself go to this extent. He banged his fist on the armrest as he chanted, "Down with turkey bacon! Down with the faux piggyarchy!"

Sabrina danced around the small sleeper car, pumping her fist in the air, in rhythm to his chant. She giggled again, and then grabbed her toiletries and some clothes before heading to the bathroom to change quickly. When she returned, dressed in a teal pantsuit, her hair was perfectly coiffed, and her makeup subtle but flattering. She knew she looked as stunning as she felt, when she sensed, before she even saw, his gaze upon her. While she had been in the bathroom, he had quickly changed into Dockers, a white and teal-striped button-down shirt, and Skechers sneakers. They looked like a couple, and Sabrina found herself secretly happy about this observation.

They proceeded to the dining car happily, once again engrossed in learning about each other. They enjoyed mimosas at a table by the window as they devoured way too much bacon (extra crispy), scrambled eggs, and biscuits. Once again, their orders matched exactly. Morning passed into afternoon seamlessly, with only a change of location to the lounge car to mark the passage of time. They were so wrapped up in each other that they almost missed the announcement that they would be arriving in Clarksville at 7 p.m. A look of disappointment crossed both their faces as they contemplated their separation.

"Wow. That trip went by so fast. I appreciate you filling the time for me. So... what are your plans this week? Are you staying with a friend or one of the hotels in town?" Sabrina asked, trying to sound nonchalant.

"Oh, let me see. I don't have any specific plans. I was thinking about maybe ice fishing, exploring the town, maybe going on a hike, ice skating... everything, really. I'm staying at this little bed and breakfast... ummm, Fireside Lodge... no, Fireside Cottage."

Sabrina broke into a wide grin.

"That's my friend's place. I'm staying there, too. I don't have any specific plans myself, other than relaxing and having some fun for once. I just thought maybe you might want to hang out a little more—that is if you are interested. I was planning to go to dinner at a cozy, little restaurant my friend recommended, The Lakeside Café. Would you care to join me?"

Jeremiah nodded eagerly.

Both of them hurriedly repacked their suitcases, eager to resume their visit in town. They were the first ones in line to exit the train as it pulled into the station, where Jeremiah had scheduled an Uber to pick them up at 7:15.

He loaded their bags into the trunk and jumped in after Sabrina. He reached down to lay his hand on the seat but accidentally placed it on hers instead. He was pleasantly surprised to find that neither of them pulled back.

Dinner seemed to pass in the blink of an eye, even though they were at the restaurant for more than two hours drinking wine and talking. They shared another Uber to the B&B, and he carried their bags up to the check-in desk.

Sabrina's friend Melanie looked up from behind the counter, shocked to see her standing there with a man. Sabrina ignored her friend's questioning looks and stepped back to let Jeremiah check in first. He signed the paperwork, grabbed his key, and then said an awkward goodnight before heading up the stairs.

Sabrina quickly told her friend she would explain everything in the morning and feigned sleepiness to speed up the process, then grabbed her bags and headed up the stairs to her room—which, she realized, was right across the hall from Jeremiah's. As she was unlocking the door, she heard his door open behind her. She hid her smile behind her hair as she realized he had been watching or listening for her.

Jeremiah held out a slip of paper as he said, "Here. I wanted to give you my number. Give me a call if you want to hang out."

Sabrina grabbed the paper in one hand and held out the other, as she asked for his phone. When he handed it to her, she quickly programmed her number into his contacts list.

"There. You can call me anytime. Have a good night."

She whisked herself away into the room, floating on air. She pressed her back to the door as she closed it and breathed deeply. Her head was spinning with all her thoughts about him... about them.

What the hell? Us! There can be no us. I have too much school to finish. A career to develop. Besides, he essentially has a fiancée. He can protest all he wants from the safety of his vacation. But could he... would he really turn his back on everything that was waiting for him back home?

Sabrina unloaded the contents of her suitcase into the bureau and laid out her toiletries on the bathroom sink. She was exhausted by the activity of the day and all the confusing feelings running through her body. She climbed into bed wearily and burrowed into a blanket cocoon. Her eyes had barely closed before she entered a restless sleep, interrupted by dreams of a life with Jeremiah.

II.

Sabrina awoke early the next morning, knowing Melanie would pounce on her as soon as she had a free moment. She headed down to breakfast with a feeling of trepidation, and as she rounded the corner, she heard Melanie talking excitedly about her to someone.

She never expected that someone to be Jeremiah.

She walked up casually as if she hadn't overheard them. They both looked up sheepishly and said good morning.

Melanie quickly rose from the table and rushed into the kitchen, mumbling about getting her breakfast ready. Jeremiah stood up and gave Sabrina a hug, then held her chair as she sat down.

"I trust you slept well. Your friend has the most luxurious beds here. How are you this morning?"

"Oh yes, I slept fine," Sabrina mumbled, stifling a yawn. "How about you?"

Jeremiah nodded. Then he reached out and casually gripped her hand, smiling as her fingers curled around his.

"I was wondering if you would like to go for a hike around the lake in a bit. Then I thought maybe we could go ice skating afterward. I will ply you with hot chocolate and Bailey's," he offered with a wink.

"Well, you certainly know the way to my heart, or at least my stomach—the one who's really in charge. I would love to go. When and where shall we meet?"

"Why don't you eat your breakfast and catch up with your friend? Then go bundle up because it is quite chilly out there today. I will meet you in the lobby at noon. Sound good?"

"Yes, of course."

Jeremiah rose and bustled out of the room, a man on a mission it seemed. Just then, Melanie returned from the kitchen with a steaming plate of food. They quickly jumped into a rapid-fire discussion about their lives the past few months. They had met in their junior year of high school and quickly became friends. They were the kind of friends who might not interact for months but would pick up their conversation again as if they'd never skipped a beat.

Finally, the moment Sabrina had been dreading arrived.

"So....?"

"So what?"

"You know what. How did you meet Jeremiah? And when? What's the story? I want some tea... spill it."

"Oh, stop! There is no tea. We met on the train to Clarksville. There was a mix-up, and we were booked into the same sleeper car. We just enjoyed each other's company on the train, and then we went to dinner afterward. We're just friends."

Melanie nodded with a knowing smile as she said, "Sure."

Sabrina looked at her watch and was relieved to see it was time to get ready. She excused herself and jogged happily up to her room. She put on her thermals under her sweats, donned her coat, then grabbed a scarf, knit hat, and gloves, which she tucked into her coat pockets. She stuffed her wallet into the other coat pocket and zipped it closed. She headed down the stairs, gaining more pep in her step as Jeremiah came into view.

He held his arm out, and she accepted it readily. Arms linked, they headed out the door, and she was surprised to see a horse-drawn carriage sitting out front.

Jeremiah led her up to the steps to mount the carriage and stiffened his arm to support her as she climbed in. He climbed in beside her and reached across to the other seat, grabbing a blanket to spread across their laps—and revealing a beautiful bouquet of roses underneath, which he presented to her with a smile. Then he grabbed a metal thermos and two mugs that were tucked into a basket on the floor.

"I promised hot chocolate with Bailey's, did I not?"

He poured two steaming, full cups and handed one to her.

She closed her eyes and moaned, "Mmmmmm!"

The carriage lurched forward as the horses began pulling on the reins, and they arrived at the park entrance about twenty minutes later.

The day was a whirlwind of activity. Occasional snow showers fell, but a full canopy of large coniferous trees protected them on the path, which wove its way through the forest and around a lake.

As the afternoon skies cleared, they arrived at the pier on the far side. A small cabin near the shore advertised "Snacks, hot and cold drinks, kayaks, and winter sports equipment rentals." So they walked up to the pull-down window on the side, where Jeremiah rented two pairs of skates.

For the next two hours, they skated around the lake, at times racing each other, and at other times pretending they were Olympic pairs skaters. The laughs and merriment flowed freely. When they were done, they began the slow, romantic stroll back around the lake to catch their ride back to the B&B. For the return trip, the carriage driver chose a slower route over winding roads with trees looming overhead.

Sabrina leaned against Jeremiah's chest, her head on his shoulder, as she looked into his eyes, lost in deep conversations that drifted from one topic to the next. Jeremiah leaned down and kissed her softly, their lips grabbing each other and then slowly pulling apart. His hand caressed her cheek softly and then slipped into her hair behind her ear, softly pulling her face closer to his. He covered her face in soft kisses from the tip of her nose to the middle of her forehead. She wrapped her arms around him and pulled him close, turning her body to put her legs across his lap.

When the carriage came to an abrupt stop, they realized that they had arrived at the B&B. They climbed out, and Jeremiah tipped the driver before they walked inside, hand in hand, unable to break eye contact. Melanie saw them enter, but she left the room surreptitiously to avoid intruding. Jeremiah walked Sabrina to her room, then swept her into his arms, kissing her passionately, before bidding her goodnight. The perfect gentleman to the very last moment.

Sabrina drifted into her room in a fog and flopped on the bed with a sigh. She had never experienced a moment like this. She had only been on a few dates in her life—only at the insistence of a friend or family member, and never seriously. Was this love or simple infatuation? Whatever it was, she wasn't sure she wanted it to end. Exhausted by the day, she fell asleep where she had dropped, her mind filled with possibilities.

The next morning, she rose early, eager to get down to breakfast and see if Jeremiah was up as well. She dressed quickly and bounced down the stairs like a teenager. A huge smile spread across her face as she saw him sitting at the table, seemingly waiting for her arrival. He motioned her over immediately and rose to help her into her seat.

"How are you this morning, Beautiful?"

"Perfect. I am feeling absolutely perfect. How are you, fine sir?" she asked with a giggle.

"Great. What would you like to do today? Or, I'm sorry... do you have plans today already?"

"Just whatever you have planned for us. Umm... I mean... umm, that is, if you wanted to spend the day together," she stammered with a blush.

"Of course. I thought we would eat breakfast here. Then we can stroll through the downtown shopping district and catch some lunch at one of the restaurants there. They're having a Christmas festival today, with a tree lighting in the town square this evening at 7. We can go eat roasted chestnuts, drink hot chocolate until we're sick, make our own Christmas ornament or wreath... There will be carolers, games, ice skating in a rink they set up near the tree, and just about any other Christmas activity you could imagine in a quaint small town. I thought it might be fun." He said it all in a breathless rush.

Sabrina giggled, delighted by his enthusiasm.

"That sounds enchanting."

Melanie had been listening through the kitchen door and rushed to bring out their breakfast. They ate ravenously, in a rush to begin the day's activities.

Sabrina ran upstairs to grab her coat and purse as Jeremiah ordered an Uber to take them into town. They waited in the lobby in the oversized armchairs by the fireplace as they watched for the car to arrive. Both of them were trying to play it cool, but anyone could see they were falling in love. The adoring looks on their faces as they stared at each other spoke volumes.

They rushed out to the car when it arrived, and Jeremiah opened the car door for her. She had never experienced such a polite man before. When they arrived downtown a short time later, they eagerly began Christmas shopping for their friends and family.

Sabrina explained that she bought a special ornament for Melanie each year because Christmas and decorations meant so much to her. They went through every shop in town, each one cuter than the last, until they found just the right one: a small snow globe containing a house, that looked just like her B&B, complete with a welcome mat out front.

Their feet were tired, and they both needed a rest after their epic shopping spree, so they headed off to lunch at Rachel's Place. The menu was full of delicious-sounding home-cooked meals. After much discussion, they both ordered open-face hot turkey sandwiches with gravy and homemade cranberry sauce. Jeremiah excused himself, explaining that he wanted to run back to a store for a moment to pick up a present he had seen for his mother.

Sabrina was watching the snow fall out the window when she saw him coming back. But instead of returning to join her, he suddenly ducked into the jewelry store. She tried to suppress a pang of jealousy, worried that he might be buying a gift for his girlfriend back home. But when he came back a short while later, he wasn't carrying a bag from the jeweler, so she pushed it out of her mind.

He excitedly showed her his purchase, inspired by the ornament they'd chosen for Melanie. His mother had a collection of large snow globes on a shelf in the living room, so he'd bought her a light-up globe in the shape of a lantern with a scene from a town (which looked remarkably like Clarksville) decorated for Christmas. It swirled with snowflakes and iridescent glitter.

After lunch, Jeremiah found a bench near one of the fire pits set up throughout downtown for people to enjoy. They talked about how much they both loved the quiet, simple life they had found in Clarksville. Yet, it was only an hour's drive from a large city if they wanted more excitement or anything they couldn't find in town. The time passed quickly, and the cold set in, so Jeremiah joined a large line waiting for hot chocolate at a food truck.

Sabrina quickly snuck away and ran into the store behind her. She had seen a fancy artist's valise with a set of professional-grade colored pencils, pastels, and a pen set in a carved wooden box displaying the train entering Clarksville. During one of their many conversations, he'd told her how much he enjoyed art—but that his father had discouraged him from pursuing it when he became a teenager. This gift would allow him to relax and explore his passion, and she just knew he would love it. She managed to get back to the bench before he noticed she had left.

The rest of the day they enjoyed all the activities throughout the square. They decided to make an ornament, rather than a wreath. Without even discussing it first, each of them made an ornament for the other.

They skated on the ice rink hand in hand to the music of a live band.

They played all the games, and Sabrina even beat him at cornhole. She had an uncanny aim with the beanbag.

After the tree lighting, the main street closed and was transformed into a giant dance floor. They danced until they realized the music had ended some time ago and nearly everyone had departed.

Even then, they still weren't ready for the night to be over, so they walked hand-in-hand the mile back to the B&B.

They quietly entered the darkened building and made their way across the lobby and up the stairs. Jeremiah wrapped his arms around Sabrina as she hurriedly unlocked her door. They entered the room and immediately embraced, kissing each other hungrily. Tired as they were after the day's fun, they did not sleep that night, which they spent making love and lying in each other's arms. They whispered deep into the night, proclaiming their love for each other and making plans for the future.

Jeremiah would go home and explain that he was willing to work at his father's company for the next four or five years, but with stipulations: He would need time off to visit Sabrina at college and then medical school, and to travel the world as he dreamed. He would make him understand that Amber was a great girl, but not the one for him. He appreciated his parents' offer to buy them a home, but he wanted to marry Sabrina and buy their own home that they chose together. Most difficult of all, he would need to have that same discussion with Amber.

Sabrina made sure he understood the depth of her need for a serious career, which meant she might not ever want a family, or at least might need to delay it for quite some time. Jeremiah did want a family, if possible, but most important to him was a life with

Sabrina. He was not in a hurry for a family anyhow. They finally fell asleep as dawn arrived, satisfied that they had charted out their future.

III.

Around 9 a.m., Sabrina awoke to Jeremiah getting dressed. He told her to go back to sleep; that he would return in a short while. He needed to call his parents because he had looked at his phone and seen multiple missed calls from the night before. He was going to take a quick shower, get dressed, and make his call; then he would return with breakfast for both of them.

At noon, Sabrina woke again to the sound of the 12 resounding bongs from the grandfather clock down the hall. She was surprised to see Jeremiah had not returned. She dressed quickly and headed down to the lobby. Melanie had saved some breakfast for her, so she sat in the dining room, facing out toward the lobby, so she could see if Jeremiah came down. Melanie hadn't seen him all day, so Sabrina became a bit concerned. She spent the next several minutes regaling Melanie with stories of the magical few days she had just spent with him. She looked up, laughing, when Jeremiah entered the room, but her smile faded at the grim look on his face.

Melanie excused herself quickly as Jeremiah approached.

"What's wrong? Are you OK?" Sabrina asked as she jumped up to embrace him.

"Please sit down. We need to talk."

Sabrina slumped in her chair, tears already forming in her eyes.

"My father had a heart attack."

"Oh my God! I am so sorry. Is he OK?"

"Yes, he is stable for now. He is going into surgery shortly for a triple bypass. I need to go home to be with my family and help my mother. But we need to talk first."

Wh... what about?" Sabrina asked as her lower lip trembled

"My mother told me my father has been very stressed out about my life choices. Apparently, I made it clearer than I thought that I am not necessarily interested in taking over his company. He is concerned about 'my questionable dedication to work.' He is also disappointed that I am here on vacation at Christmas, rather than home proposing to my girlfriend, so we can start a family. My mom blames me for his health issues. She's afraid that if I don't come home now and stop being so 'selfish' about my own needs... he will die."

"OK. I understand you need to be with your family now. We can see each other again soon. Maybe you can visit me at Stanford in a few weeks. I will make time..." Sabrina trailed off as she saw a tear fall onto his chest.

"Sabrina, dear Sabrina. If only... if only I could. My father is demanding and controlling, but he really is a good man. I cannot disappoint him. He has been planning for me to take over for my entire life. At one time, when I was young, I thought I wanted that too, so it's probably my fault for encouraging him. As much as what I want matters, I cannot be responsible for my father dying. I cannot destroy my family. I couldn't handle that."

"OK, I understand. You need to go home and take over for your dad right now while he recovers. I will be busy with my externships, finishing college, and then especially with medical school over the next four years. But we can keep in contact. I will wait for you. We can figure all this out with time. There are some amazing hospitals in Los Angeles. Maybe I can apply for a residency at USC Medical Center. They have a top-rated program."

The tears fell faster, as he silently began to shake his head no.

"I will not let you wait for me. You are far too special to waste your life on me. Go back to school, thrive, and most importantly, let yourself live. You deserve it. You are more than honoring your mother's memory. She would never want you to devote yourself solely to work. She would want you happy, just as I do. Promise me!"

"I could never do that. I never wanted to love someone... to get married. It was you, only you that could have ever changed my mind. I can't do this."

Sabrina jumped up from the table, sobbing, as she ran up the stairs. She threw herself on the bed and let the tears flow. She cried her heart out as she mourned the life she could have had, almost as strongly as she still mourned the loss of her mother.

Later that afternoon, as she was staring at the wall in a daze, she heard a light knock on the door and Melanie's voice calling out to her.

She opened the door and fell into her friend's arms, crying uncontrollably once again. Melanie told her that Jeremiah had gone for a walk hours ago, looking broken, and had not returned yet. She tried to console Sabrina, but she didn't know what to say. She promised to bring up some dinner later and finally persuaded her to lie back down and rest in the meantime.

Sabrina remembered the Christmas present she had gotten him. As heartbroken as she was, she still loved him and wished him the best. She grabbed it off the dresser and quickly ran out, setting it against his door where he wouldn't miss it. Then she returned to her room to nap after putting up the Do Not Disturb sign. The sun was dipping in the sky when she awoke to insistent knocking at her door. A quick look out the peephole revealed it was Jeremiah, bags in hand. She couldn't face him again, so she quietly crept back away from the door. He begged her to answer, but she pretended to be gone.

Finally, the knocking stopped.

About half an hour later, she once again heard knocking, followed this time by Melanie's voice. She opened the door to find her standing there with an enormous BLT.

Melanie smiled sheepishly and said, "I didn't know what else I could do to make you happy."

Sabrina cried through her tears and thanked her friend. She found she was hungry after all. Apparently, that much sorrow and tears built up an appetite. Melanie quietly sat with her while she ate, letting her decide if and when she was ready to talk. Sabrina forced herself to engage in small talk and then told Melanie she was ready for bed. She promised to be up early the next morning for Christmas. Melanie turned at the door, seeming unsure about whether to speak or not. Finally, she reached down and grabbed an object off the side table in the hall.

She held out her hand gingerly as she whispered, "He left a few minutes after you didn't answer the door to him. He gave this to me and begged me to make sure you got it. He said it was important that you accept it."

Sabrina frowned but reached out to grab it from her.

"Thank you."

The next day was as dark and gloomy as she felt, with snow falling heavily outside. Her friend was ecstatic for a white Christmas, but all she noticed was the stormy weather that matched the way she felt inside. They had a wonderful breakfast with cinnamon rolls, bacon, eggs, and eggnog... heavily spiked eggnog. Afterward, they opened the presents, and Melanie was brought to tears when she received her ornament. Sabrina excused herself for a moment and went upstairs to get the present Jeremiah had left. She couldn't bear to open it alone. She tore off the paper to reveal a small purple box emblazoned with the jewelry store logo.

He went to the jewelry store for me?

She slowly opened the box to reveal a white gold necklace with two intertwined hearts. The intersecting sides of the two hearts were connected with a double helix, like DNA. The tears poured from her eyes, as she read the small handwritten note tucked inside the box:

We are two complementary strands of the same structure, inseparable soulmates. Truly, you will hold my heart forever, my angel.

Melanie helped her put on the necklace after reading the note.

He will hold my heart forever, too.

The two friends enjoyed each other's company for the rest of the day as they ate way too much of the delicious food that Melanie made for dinner and dessert. Eventually, they fell asleep on the couch watching Christmas movies.

The next day, Sabrina got up and slowly packed for her trip home to Stanford. Melanie drove her to the train station and stayed with her until it was time to board. She had bought some snacks and drinks at the convenience store on the way to the station. She wanted to be able to hole up in her sleeper car alone and not leave until she arrived.

The train ride passed quickly, in a blur of sleeping and staring aimlessly out the window. Sabrina frequently found her fingers running along the hearts, tracing the design, as she silently cried.

Once home, Sabrina jumped into her externship with utter devotion. Every free moment was spent at the hospital, even long after her shift had ended.

Those two weeks passed quickly, and she was given a glowing review, just as she had hoped. She then returned to school and immersed herself in her studies with the same single-minded determination to excel.

P=2ℓ+2

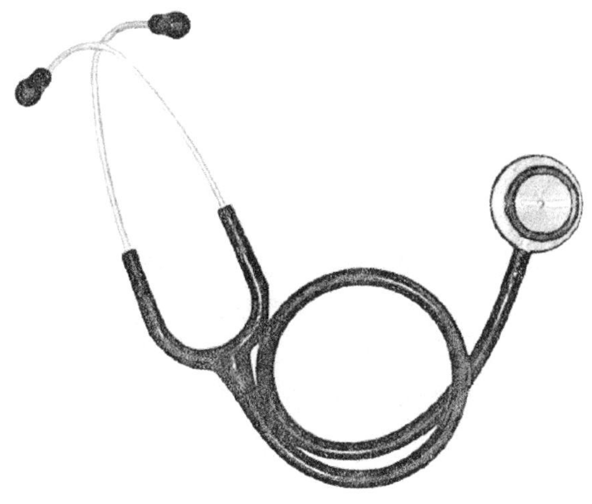

IV.

About a month after the semester started, she received a call one evening. Her mouth dropped open when she heard Jeremiah's voice on the other end of the line.

"Sabrina, please don't hang up. How are you doing?"

"I am doing fine," she stated emphatically, although she truly did not feel that way.

"I miss you. I know you probably don't believe that, but I do. More than you could possibly know."

Against her will, she found herself saying, "I do, too."

"How is school going?"

"It is going well. My externship went perfectly. How is your life going? How is your father? Did you marry her? I am sorry. None of that is my business."

"No, it is fine. We always told each other everything... even from the first moment we met. My father is getting better. He has returned to work full time. I am still running the company for him. No, I am not married. But... I am engaged. I am supposed to get married on June 1st."

Sabrina gulped audibly.

"I am happy for you... if that is what you want."

"Do you really feel that way? Do you not care at all anymore? Would I be calling you if I were happy? I don't know what to do. I don't know how to extract myself from this situation. I don't want this. You know that!"

"Yes, I do. But what do you want me to do? How can I help you? I said I would wait for you. You couldn't make that decision. You didn't choose me."

"I know, I know. I was stupid and wrong. Can we keep in touch and see where this goes? Can you ever forgive me? Do you even still love me? Do you want to be with me?"

"I love you more than YOU could possibly know. It is all I have wanted since that night we spent together. I forgave you that same day you left, even though my heart was broken. I could never be with anyone else but you."

Sabrina and Jeremiah spent hours on the phone that night going over all the details of their lives during the previous two months. The call ended slowly, with great reluctance to let each other go, after many proclamations of love.

The next months were filled with calls and emails. Every spare moment they had was spent with each other. Neither of them had ever been so happy . In those emails, they resumed planning their life together. Their correspondence was filled with details of their hopes for the future. But they were also filled with Jeremiah's concerns about how his father and fiancée would handle the news. Before they knew it, Sabrina's graduation had arrived.

She was surprised to see Jeremiah sitting there, front and center, cheering her on the whole time she crossed the stage. He whistled and clapped louder than anyone else at the conclusion of her speech; she had graduated top of her class, just as she had hoped, so she'd been chosen to give the commencement address.

He joined her briefly at the party afterward, then they quickly went back to her apartment to spend a blissful night together, making love passionately, as if it were both their first and last time together.

Afterward, they lay in each other's arms discussing the plans for the coming week. Sabrina would be busy packing up her belongings and moving into the new apartment they planned to share close to the medical school. Then she had a lot of loose ends to tie up before her summer externship and medical school orientation. After she finished all that, she had one glorious week of free time to return to Clarksville for a romantic vacation with Jeremiah.

He was going to spend this week explaining his change of heart to his parents and Amber. Then he needed to pack up his belongings so he could move them into their apartment after they returned from vacation. He had interviews scheduled at some architectural firms in the area for the week after their return. They were both going to be so busy in the week ahead that they knew they probably wouldn't have time to contact each other, so they soaked up every moment together that night.

As expected, the week passed in a flurry of activity, and Sabrina dropped into bed exhausted each night. Monday, her day of departure, arrived before she knew it. She excitedly boarded the train and passed the time reading from some of her new textbooks, which she had picked up the day before. She would arrive in Clarksville on the morning train Wednesday, and then wait there for Jeremiah to arrive on the 4:30 train.

Melanie surprised her by meeting her at the station upon her arrival. They walked the short distance into downtown and had breakfast together as she waited. Melanie was dying to hear all the news about their reconciliation. She was thrilled to see Sabrina so happy and fulfilled. Afterward, they had coffee together as they sat on a bench and watched the children playing in the park. Melanie had to return to the B&B because she was expecting guests, so Sabrina walked back to the station.

She anxiously waited for the next few hours until the train's arrival, literally popping out of her seat when she heard the whistle blow as it pulled into the station. The passengers disembarked quickly, and her anxiety grew as Jeremiah failed to appear. Ten minutes later, all the passengers seemed to have disembarked. Sabrina ran up to the conductor to ask if anyone was still on the train, and he replied no. Then she ran over to the ticket counter to see if they could find out if he had boarded the train. A short search on the computer showed his ticket had not been used, nor had it been rescheduled, at least not yet.

Sabrina tried to calm herself as she sat on the bench outside the station and called Jeremiah. The phone rang six times before it went through to voicemail. When it did, she tried to sound calm: She didn't want to reveal her actual level of fear and anger.

"Hey, Jeremiah! How are you doing, sweetie? I am here at the station, and they say you didn't get on the train. Is everything OK? I will wait to hear from you and meet you at the station tomorrow, I guess. Call me. I love you."

She needed to work through her feelings, so she walked back to Melanie's B&B. When she walked in the door and saw Melanie's face, all her feelings burst through the dam she had so carefully constructed.

"Calm down, Sabrina. You don't know what happened. He may just be running late. Maybe he took a plane instead and will arrive here later tonight or in the morning. You need to wait to hear from him."

"He backed out. I just know it. He was so afraid of how they would all handle it. He just doesn't have the guts to break my heart again in person."

"Now, you don't know that. I don't believe that's true. He may be a people pleaser when it comes to his family, but he truly does love you, too. There is no way he would not let you know if he changed his mind. He would call or email you or something. I honestly believe that."

As the hours passed with no word, her depression grew. The hours turned into days, and still she heard nothing. On the first day, she came downstairs to eat and watch television or play card games with Melanie. She left dozens of messages, but not one was returned. On the second day, she just stayed in bed with the blinds closed. She slept most of the day, barely ate, and rarely spoke to

Melanie when she came to check on her. The day before she was due to leave, Melanie literally dragged Sabrina out of bed and into a warm shower. She helped her dress and led her downstairs to lunch, where she spoon-fed her soup until she finally started eating on her own.

Soon, the tears began to flow again. Then, after a few minutes, the sorrow turned into anger. While Melanie felt bad for her, she was at least glad to see her reacting again.

"That is it. I am done. We are done. I am not going to let him fuck with my head again. He can't change his mind in a few months, and come back to me again," she yelled as she pulled her phone out of her pocket.

She promptly blocked his phone number and deleted him from her contacts and on social media.

"Thank you for taking care of me, Melanie. You are a true friend. I'm sorry I was so much trouble. Now I need to go pack and see if I can cancel my train ticket, so I can just fly home instead and have a couple of days before my externship starts. Apparently, I need to move again, because I am not going to run into him at that apartment we rented."

Sabrina was all packed up and back downstairs an hour later. She had gotten a refund for the train ticket and found a flight scheduled to leave in three hours, leaving her just enough time to get to the airport.

She hugged Melanie tight to her and promised she would call when she got home. A short time later, her Uber arrived, and Sabrina was on her way.

Sabrina stayed at the Hilton by the airport that night and began to search online in earnest to find a new apartment. When she called a few places in the morning, she was happy to find one she could afford that would let her move in that weekend.

Then she lost no time in taking a bus over to the apartment she had planned to share with Jeremiah, where she went immediately to see the property manager. He grudgingly removed her name from the lease, but only after she agreed to pay a two-month penalty and forfeit her deposit. She was grateful, looking back, that she had been in such a rush before leaving on her trip, so she hadn't unpacked much. Moving would mostly be a matter of just transferring her boxes from one apartment to the next.

Once again, Sabrina dove into her externship. This time, it was much more involved because she had proved her merit during Christmas break. The months passed quickly, and soon it was time to start medical school. Sabrina had always been an exceptional student, but medical school was challenging, as she had expected. She welcomed that challenge, though, because it gave her very little time to feel sorry for herself.

As she started her third year in school, she began her clinical rotations in the school clinic and at the hospital. She had very little free time anyhow, but she found she was thinking of Jeremiah less and less.

All that truly mattered was that Sabrina had learned her lesson. She had been right to never want marriage or a family. Her career was all that mattered to her. There was no longer anything holding her there, so she applied for a residency in emergency medicine at Johns Hopkins Hospital. As the fourth year came closer to the end, she began to get anxious as she waited to hear if she had been accepted.

Finally, word came in and, based on glowing recommendations from the doctor in charge of her externships, her professors, and the doctors overseeing her clinicals, she was accepted.

She graduated from medical school, once again at the top of her class. The next few weeks were insanely busy as she packed all her belongings and had them shipped across the country. She had to make a trip early to find an apartment near the hospital because she knew she'd be working long hours and didn't want a long commute on top of that. She didn't need anything special because she was expecting to sleep in the on-call room frequently.

Melanie came to visit before her move and helped her pack. It was going to be difficult to be so far from her, but they intended to use Zoom to keep in touch as often as possible.

Sabrina drove across the country as quickly as she could. She wanted a few days to get settled before beginning her rigorous residency. Sabrina worked long shifts at the hospital and volunteered for overtime or took on other people's shifts as often as possible. Her dedication to her training impressed her supervisors, who could tell she was studying emergency medicine procedures in her free time. Not surprisingly, in her second year, she was chosen as Chief Resident to serve in that position in years three and four. Those years passed quickly, and she applied to be an attending physician after graduation.

Sabrina was readily accepted for the position. She was an excellent doctor and well-liked by her colleagues, nurses, and support staff. The years passed quickly, and after five years, she was a shoo-in for the Chief of Emergency Medicine position when her boss retired. Sabrina was over the moon when she found out she had finally landed her dream job, especially at such a prestigious hospital as Johns Hopkins. Her days were long and hard, especially when she began a research project. She was hoping to get published in the near future.

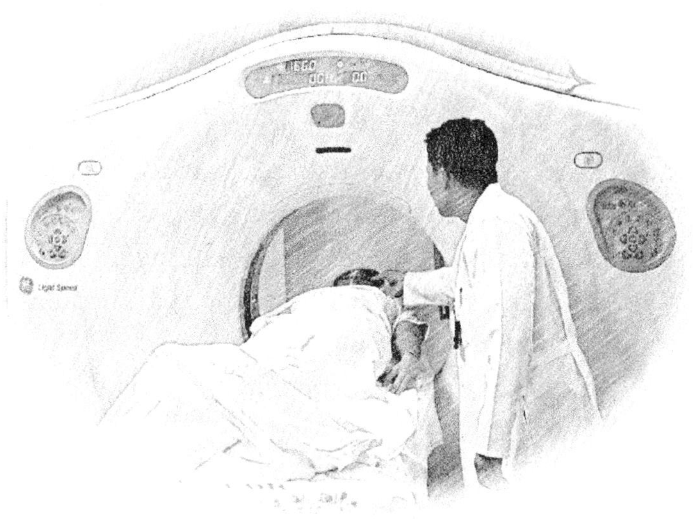

V.

Sabrina wasn't shocked when she began having gastrointestinal issues. Between her rapidly approaching research deadline and her long hours in the Emergency Department, she was under enormous pressure. Her terrible diet didn't help either. She was prone to eating whatever was quick and convenient as she rushed from one emergency to the next. When she actually had the time to leave the hospital, she frequently bought fast food on the way home.

Sabrina started to become concerned when the frequent heartburn continued to worsen, even after she started taking medication. Her symptoms soon progressed to frequent nausea and occasional vomiting. When the stomach pain started, she thought she had developed an ulcer. It wasn't until her symptoms became debilitating that she finally scheduled an appointment with a colleague in the gastroenterology department. The doctor scheduled an ultrasound first.

Sabrina became very concerned as she lay on the table and looked over at the screen. There was plainly a mass effect in her stomach. The ultrasound technician feigned ignorance, but it was clear that she was concerned as well. Dr. Burrows called her office that evening and explained he had scheduled her for an endoscopy the following week. He told her not to worry, but she knew better.

Besides, she could hear the worried tone in his voice.

"I don't have time next week. My research project wraps up late this week, and I need to write up my findings. Then, next week, I have a new crop of residents entering the program, and you know I like to be hands-on with them the first few weeks."

"Dr. Sanders... Sabrina, this is serious. We cannot afford to wait. I need you to do this for me.

You know as well as I do that a CT is a quick procedure. Make time."

"OK. Thank you, Bob. I appreciate your candor and concern. I will do my best to make the appointment Thursday."

The following week passed even faster than she had expected. Her new residents were greener than she had hoped, so they needed even more supervision. It wasn't until late Thursday night, when she received a call from Bob, that she remembered she had missed her appointment.

"I'm very sorry, Bob. I do take this seriously. I will call the scheduling department and get in as soon as possible."

"Please do, Sabrina. I am serious here."

A week later, Sabrina finally called the scheduling department. She booked her CT for the end of the month when her schedule was a little lighter. Truth be told, Sabrina was scared. Given her family history and what she'd seen on the ultrasound screen, she wasn't sure she wanted to know what they would find. But she realized she couldn't put it off any longer. The symptoms, especially the pain, were becoming intolerable. It was very difficult to eat, and she was losing enough weight that people were beginning to ask questions with concern in their eyes.

Finally, the day of the CT arrived. She barely made it to the appointment, but she did get it done. She ran off to the Emergency Department as soon as she was finished and avoided the computer as much as possible, actively trying to keep from seeing the results when they arrived. Bob—or, as she would refer to him here on out, Dr. Burrows—called around lunchtime and asked her to stop by as soon as possible.

Sabrina finally convinced herself to go down to his office in the late afternoon. When she entered his office, she knew the news was going to be just as she expected.

"I am very sorry to tell you this, Sabrina, but a large area of your stomach lining appears abnormal. With suspicious tissue of this type and size, there is an 80 percent chance of malignancy. Given your family history, I am highly suspicious that you have diffuse gastric adenocarcinoma. Frequently, at this size, it will have already metastasized to either your liver or lungs. There are suspicious-looking spots in your liver and what appears to be metastasis to your lungs. I have scheduled surgery for you at 8 a.m. tomorrow. I have already talked to your boss and explained the situation. I need you to go downstairs and check into the hospital now. Do you understand?"

Sabrina opened her mouth to argue, but then just nodded her head.

"I will see you in the morning, Dr. Burrows."

Sabrina walked down the hall, head spinning with the news she had just received. She went to Admitting, where they helped her quickly and compassionately.

Clearly, they had been expecting her.

One of the nurses on duty, Nurse Andrews, met her and escorted her up to her room. They chatted casually as she changed into her hospital gown, had her IV put in, and settled into bed. Nurse Andrews asked if she needed anything before she left, and then reminded her that she may want to call someone and let them know about the situation.

Melanie was the only person Sabrina could think of to contact. When she heard, she was devastated by the news and offered to help in any way she could.

"I'm fine. I will be fine," Sabrina told her. "This is just a scare. I am sure everything will be okay. I just didn't want you to worry if I missed our weekly Zoom session. I will call you tomorrow when I'm out of recovery."

Sabrina settled in and finally dropped off to real sleep shortly before 5 a.m. She was awakened two hours later when the nurse came in to prepare her for surgery.

She was shocked when she opened her eyes and found Melanie sitting by her side.

"Melanie! I told you not to come. What about your B&B?"

"I didn't have any reservations for this week anyhow. I closed it. I have a friend who will check messages and go by to make sure everything is fine. There is no place else I could or would be right now. Now quit worrying about me and get ready to fight. That is your only concern."

Sabrina awoke from surgery, once again in her room, and found Melanie by her side talking to Dr. Burrows.

"Well, hello there, Sabrina. Are you OK? Do you feel up to talking?"

Sabrina nodded solemnly.

"I removed a sample of your stomach lining and had stat pathology performed while you were under. It came back as I suspected, so I had to remove 60 percent of your stomach. I removed over a dozen lymph nodes, and they all came back positive for adenocarcinoma. I then performed a biopsy of one of the suspicious patches on your liver. It also tested positive. I am afraid you have advanced Stage 4 gastric adenocarcinoma with metastasis to your liver and lungs. I need to see you back in my office in two weeks to assess the status of your healing. In the meantime, I will get you scheduled as soon as possible to have a port inserted for chemotherapy. Fingers crossed, in two weeks, we will begin an aggressive course of chemotherapy for the next three months and then reassess your staging with another CT. Do you have any questions?"

"Let's cut the crap, Dr. Burrows. We both know what we are talking about here. What is my long-term prognosis?"

"Sabrina, I will not tell you that it is hopeless, but I will not tell you that everything is going to be fine either. I will give it to you straight. The five-year survival rate is less than 20 percent with genetic diffuse gastric adenocarcinoma. It all depends on your response to chemotherapy."

"Thank you, Dr. Burrows."

Melanie crawled into bed with Sabrina and just held her. There was nothing to say. They each knew that all they could do was support each other. Melanie stayed for the next week through the hardest part of Sabrina's recovery from surgery. She left reluctantly—and only at Sabrina's insistence when she threatened to end their friendship if she stayed. Sabrina spent the next week at home watching television and reading. At her appointment, she was told her healing was adequate and she could begin chemo later that week.

"Aggressive chemotherapy" didn't begin to describe Sabrina's experience. Her nausea and vomiting increased to the point that she developed an ulcer in her esophagus from exposure to all the stomach acid. Eating became a chore, and her weight loss increased. She was so tired that work was impossible, so she had to take a leave of absence for three months as she proceeded through the course of treatment.

Finally, it was time for her second CT scan, to see how effective the treatment had been. Dr. Burrows scheduled it for early in the morning, and arranged for her to come in late that afternoon to go over the results.

They were not good.

In fact, they reflected the worst-case scenario: The metastasis in her lungs and liver had worsened significantly. Moreover, the cancer had continued to grow and spread through what stomach tissue remained after her surgery. Dr. Burrows explained that they could try increasing her chemo dose, but he was worried that her high level of sensitivity meant it would quickly become intolerable—and potentially life-threatening.

"Sabrina, it is time that we talk about palliative care. We need to make you more comfortable and able to enjoy the time you have left."

"I understand, Dr. Burrows. What is the next step? How long are we talking about? I want to spend what time I have left traveling, and then go visit Melanie."

"It is really hard to say, Sabrina. However, I would estimate you have between one and three months. I can get you set up with a national hospice provider that can get the medications prescribed to keep you comfortable. They have locations across the country, so if you plan your trip carefully, you should be able to find care easily as you need it."

"Thank you, Dr. Burrows."

Sabrina left the hospital and began organizing her affairs immediately. She had always been one to pursue whatever task ahead of her with stubborn independence and deep resolve. This situation was no different.

She packed a few suitcases with whatever clothes and important personal belongings she wanted to take with her. Everything else she either sold or donated to charity. She put in emergency notice with her landlord and paid him the last month's rent. She then proceeded to Johns Hopkins and submitted her resignation and said goodbye to all the colleagues who had been important to her.

She called Melanie and let her know she would be leaving in two days to drive across the country, stopping to see every historical or fascinating point of interest along the way. She then asked her the one question she had been dreading.

"I don't have long. By the time I get to you I will probably only have a matter of weeks. I have taken care of all my belongings and bills. I have made my funeral arrangements. All my assets will be passed to you, and my lawyer will take care of the probate process for you. You are the only person in my life that I want to spend my last days with. Can I stay with you?"

Melanie sniffled as she replied, "Of course. I would never forgive you if you didn't let me take care of you. I love you. You are my best friend. Please keep me apprised of your location and how you are doing as you travel. I will see you soon."

Sabrina drove slowly across the country, making stops in Washington, D.C., the Great Lakes, Mount Rushmore, Yellowstone, the Grand Canyon, Salt Lake City, and Yosemite. Sabrina was singing along to the Monkees song, "Last Train to Clarksville," as she drove down from Yosemite into the small town of Lee Vining. She was actually feeling hungry for once, so she stopped at a restaurant in a gas station that was well known there.

While she was waiting for her order, she noticed a newspaper open on a table next to hers. She saw a picture of a train, and the name "Clarksville" in the headline beside it. She grabbed it and, when she read the story quickly, she was devastated at what she learned: The train to Clarksville was being discontinued at the end of the week. While that train still held painful memories, it also was the key to the best memories of her lifetime, besides her younger years with her mother.

She called Melanie while she was eating and explained that she would be changing her plans. The trip had been getting more difficult with each passing day as she became more tired, and her pain increased. She explained to her that she was going to hire an automobile transport service to deliver her car to Melanie's B&B. She was going to catch the train and arrive in Clarksville on its last day in service. Melanie was concerned that this trip would be too painful for her, but she insisted that she needed to hold on to all her good memories, regardless of the eventual outcome.

Sabrina boarded the train, having once again paid for a private sleeper car. She enjoyed the scenery on the long ride but found herself sleeping most of the time. She ventured out to the dining car once to get a small bite to eat. Another passenger expressed concern about her when she felt woozy and grabbed onto a table to right herself as she walked back to her car. She thanked him for his concern and told him she was fine. She realized she was still feeling a tad weak, so she settled back into her seat to take a short nap before her arrival in Clarksville in approximately an hour.

Sabrina awoke with a start as the train rumbled to a halt. She saw people bustling off the train, so she slowly gathered her belongings together and began to make her way out. She thanked the conductor for his help during the trip, but he didn't hear her as he hurried by in response to a loud call from another employee. She carefully made her way down the stairs and stepped onto the platform. She looked up as a hand reached out and grabbed her bag from her.

She found herself looking into the irresistible gaze of Jeremiah.

What the hell is he doing here? And damn him! Why is it that men grow more handsome with age? He barely looks like he has aged a day.

Before she knew it, she found herself rushing into his arms, hugging him tight, as he dropped her bags at their feet. Then she sighed audibly before saying, "Hello, Jeremiah. How are you? What are you doing here?"

"I heard about the train. You know how we both love trains, and this particular one holds such fond memories for me. I had to be here for its last trip."

"Me too. I came to visit Melanie. I really need to get going. She is probably waiting for me in the station."

"Wait! I need to be honest with you. I did want to be here for the train's last arrival. But to be honest, I was hoping I would find you here. I needed to see you again. I needed to apologize and tell you how I feel. I need to beg you for one last chance."

"NO! I will not do this again. It is too late... for so many reasons. I really have to go. I cannot keep her waiting."

"She isn't here right now. I am here to pick you up. Please just hear me out on the way to the B&B. If you can't forgive me after that, I will leave you alone... forever."

"Fine. I am not up to arguing with you. Let's go."

There was some kind of issue at the station. Sabrina could hear a woman yelling, and a crowd of people was staring at her. An ambulance pulled up, so it must have been some kind of medical emergency. Jeremiah led Sabrina around the far side of the station to the parking lot, where he had a car waiting. He loaded her bags into the car and then held her door as she got in.

Well, at least he still has some of his gentlemanly manners left.

Jeremiah got in the car and backed out. He was taking the slower back roads to the B&B. She let it go because she wasn't up to arguing.

"I guess I should explain what happened that week."

"You think? Proceed. Not that I care. It is too late."

"I packed up all my belongings and stored them in a pod that was scheduled to be delivered the day after we arrived home from our trip. Then I went to my parents' house and had it out with them. My father was livid. My mother cried. They begged me to change my mind. They threatened to cut me off, and even cut me out of the will entirely. I told them that I did not need, nor want, their money. I told my father that I did not want to run his company, and that he should pass it along to his longtime, loyal employee Mark. I explained that I would be moving up to Stanford with you and finding a job there. They threatened to cut off contact with me, but I did not back down. Finally, they said that they accepted my decision, but I knew they were counting on me to come crawling back eventually when our relationship failed.

"Next, I went to Amber and explained the situation to her. She was not surprised. She knew I was unhappy and did not want to marry her. She had been waiting for just this moment to arrive. She tried to beg me to marry her, promising me to be a good wife. She swore that she would travel more and wait until I was ready for a family. I told her that this would not be a fair solution for either one of us. I explained I had no doubts she would be an excellent wife... just not for me."

"Then what happened? Why didn't you come to me? Why didn't you return my calls?"

Jeremiah pulled up in front of the B&B and turned off the car. He got out and came around to open Sabrina's door. He led her over to the garden in the backyard, and they sat down on the swing.

"That day, I was running late. I loaded my bags into the car and left in a rush to make my train. I was waiting at a long red light, and when it finally changed, I hit the gas. Unfortunately, a semi coming down the hill on the cross street lost its brakes, so the driver was unable to stop at the light. I saw him coming at me as I started across the intersection, but it was too late to stop. He slammed into the driver's side door going about 40 miles per hour. I was killed instantly. That is why I didn't come here to meet you. I couldn't. Wild horses couldn't have kept me away, but death did what I thought was impossible."

Sabrina looked at him in disbelief.

"What the hell are you talking about? Do you take me for an idiot? That is impossible. You are sitting right here, clearly not dead."

Sabrina stood up quickly and turned to leave. Jeremiah jumped up quickly and took her in his arms gently.

"Please wait. There is one more thing I need to explain to you. Please give me one more moment."

Sabrina nodded, and Jeremiah sat down again, pulling her into his lap with his arms wrapped comfortingly around her.

"I can explain why I am here telling you this. I came to meet you at the train to welcome you into the afterlife. Remember the commotion we saw at the station and the woman we heard yelling? That woman yelling was Melanie. The commotion occurred because one of the train employees found you in your sleeper car. When the conductor noticed you hadn't gotten off the train, he sent someone to find you because you'd been sick earlier. They found that you had passed away."

"That's not possible. I feel fine... perfect in fact. I can't be dead."

"Exactly, sweetie. You have not felt 'fine' in a very long time. That is your first clue that things are not as they seem to you. Follow me. I will show you."

Jeremiah stood her on her feet again. Then he got up, taking her hand, and led her into Melanie's B&B. She was not there at the front desk as she should have been. He led her up the stairs to Melanie's room, where they found her crying on the phone. Sabrina stood there quietly in front of Melanie and listened to her talk.

"Yes, sir. I am so sorry. I didn't know she hadn't told you she was sick. She was coming here to spend her final days with me. I went to the station to pick her up. She wasn't there, and when I asked about her, they told me they had called an ambulance because they couldn't find a pulse. The ambulance pronounced her dead upon arrival. I know. I can't believe it. How can she be gone?"

"Melanie! Melanie! I am right here. Please stop crying."

Sabrina reached out to hug her, but her arms passed right through her. Jeremiah grabbed her hand and led her out of the room.

"I am so sorry, sweetheart. I would never have left you alone. In fact, I didn't leave you alone. I have been with you all this time. Through your externship, the long hard years of medical school, and then all the lonely, crazy years since then. Whenever the stress started to become too much, I would find small ways to leave you messages and bring back good memories. Every time you heard 'Last Train to Clarksville,' that was me. Every time, you felt like someone was with you, that was me. Remember when you found those mysterious flowers on your front porch ?"

She nodded.

"That was me. I was always there to support you. I left that newspaper open for you on the table to find the story about the train. I needed to lead you here to me, so we could be together again... here. I needed to be the one to explain to you what had happened. Do you understand?"

"Yes... yes, I do. But what happens next?"

Jeremiah kissed her gently on the forehead, and then grabbed her hand, leading her out of the garden.

"Whatever you want, my dear. Where shall we go? What shall we do? We have eternity to love each other and do whatever our hearts desire."

Sabrina smiled and followed him down the path into town.

About the author

Sharon Marie Provost is the author of *Shadow's Gate*, *Dark Arts*, and *Shades of Love Volume 2* and co-author with Stephen H. Provost of *Christmas Nightmare's Eve* and *All Hallows' Nightmare's Eve*. Her stories have also appeared in the ACES Anthologies for 2023 and 2024, which highlight the works of Northern Nevada writers and for which she served as co-editor.

Chief operating officer of Dragon Crown Books, Sharon is a longtime resident of Carson City, where she lives with her husband and her pets. She worked for 20 years as a veterinary office manager and is the owner of champion of dog-trial poodles, and the creator of handmade dreamcatchers and chainmail jewelry. You can find her at local craft fairs, author events, and at "Sharon Marie Provost, Author" on Facebook.

Books by Sharon Marie Provost

Dark Arts: Love Me Tinder
Shades of Love Vol. 2
Shadow's Gate
All Hallows' Nightmare's Eve
(with Stephen H. Provost)
Christmas Nightmare's Eve
(with Stephen H. Provost)
The ACES Anthology 2023 & 2024
(contributor)

Did you enjoy this book?

Recommend it to a friend. And please consider **rating it and/or leaving a brief review** at Amazon, Barnes & Noble, and Goodreads.

Made in the USA
Las Vegas, NV
22 December 2024